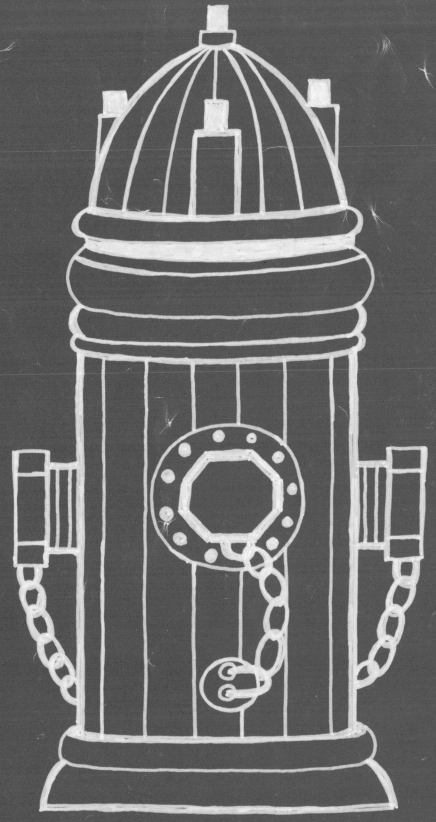

THE HOUSE

Story and pictures by
ANNE ROCKWELL

HarperCollinsPublishers

On Visitor's Day, Jason couldn't wait to
visit the firehouse. He loved fire engines.

On the big day, his friend Camilla was there, too.
Shiny red fire engines were parked in front of the
firehouse, and there were plenty of balloons.
"Come on in!" Captain Jack said.

Everyone followed him upstairs.

"This is where we wait for the alarm to ring," Captain Jack said. "We read, watch TV, play cards, sleep, lift weights, and cook. We always have good things to eat!"

Firefighters passed out lemonade and cookies shaped like fire engines.

Suddenly, the alarm rang so loudly that Jason covered his ears.

"Don't worry," said Captain Jack. "It's not a real fire. But we'll show you what we'd do if it were. Everything we need to fight fires has a place and everything is in its place. We can't waste time looking for what we need."

He slid down the pole, then jumped into his pants and boots and coat. Jason didn't know it was possible to get dressed so fast.

He wished he could
slide down the pole, too.
He imagined how much
fun that would be.

"Our clothes are fireproof and waterproof so they won't catch on fire or get wet," said Captain Jack. "The stripes glow in the dark so we can see each other in smoke and darkness."

Lieutenant Maria said, "We put on our hard helmets when we get to a fire, in case something hard falls on our heads. We wear hoses connected to air tanks on our backs so we don't breathe smoke. We pull down our helmets' fireproof ear flaps."

Captain Jack patted the side of one shiny red
fire engine proudly. "This is Engine Number One,
our pumper," he said.

"It's full of water and hoses and all the other things
we need to put out fires."

Four other firefighters climbed into the seats in
the back of the cab.

Lieutenant Maria climbed into the driver's seat
of Engine Number One. Captain Jack sat beside her.
Jason wished he could sit in the fire engine, too.
He wished he could look at everything from the
driver's seat.

pumper tank
(holds 500 gallons
of water)

revolving
spotlights

pumper controls

pike
poles

flat
hose

shovels

lanterns

axes

small tools

nozzles

air tanks

wrenches

"This is Engine Number Two, our ladder truck,"
Captain Jack said. "See the extension ladder folded up
on top of it?"

Captain Jack climbed the steps that led to the top of Engine Number Two. While he worked the controls, the extension ladder unfolded and began to go up, up, up into the sky. Then he started to climb it.

Jason watched him go higher and higher, above the roof of the firehouse, above the tall tree next door. He was sure he wouldn't be scared to climb that high if he were a real firefighter like Captain Jack.

When Captain Jack came down, he said Jason
could sit in the driver's seat of Engine Number One.
Captain Jack helped him up. The seat was high and
the steering wheel was big.

Next it was Camilla's turn. Jason didn't mind because now it was his turn to sit in the driver's seat of Engine Number Two. Jason felt just like a *real* firefighter.

When it was time to go, Jason
wore a fire helmet of his very own.
He carried a red balloon with
a picture of a fire engine on it.

As soon as Jason got home, he wanted to play with
his red toy ladder truck. But he couldn't find it.
So he got busy.

Before long the toy ladder truck was parked outside
a firehouse made of blocks. Everything was in its place.

That night Jason dreamed of beautiful big red shiny
fire engines racing through the night, lights flashing,
sirens wailing.

And he was the driver, sitting right next to Captain Jack.

For all the children
who love brave firefighters
and their beautiful fire engines

At the Firehouse
Copyright © 2003 by Anne Rockwell
Manufactured in China. All rights reserved.
www.harperchildrens.com

Library of Congress Cataloging-in-Publication Data
Rockwell, Anne F.
At the firehouse / story and pictures by Anne Rockwell.
p.   cm.
Summary: Jason, who loves fire engines, goes to the firehouse on
Visitor's Day and learns all about being a firefighter.
ISBN 0-06-029815-4 — ISBN 0-06-029816-2 (lib. bdg.)
[1. Fire departments—Fiction. 2. Fire engines—Fiction.
3. Firefighters—Fiction.] I. Title.
PZ7.R5943 Co 2003   [E]--dc21   2002006375

Typography by Elynn Cohen
1 2 3 4 5 6 7 8 9 10
❖
First Edition